PETB🐱TS

37

Having illustrated numerous children's books, Judy Brown thought it was about time that she wrote some of her own. Petbots is her third and latest series of children's novels. Judy has three children and lives in Surrey with her family and cats. You can find out all about her at www.judybrown.co.uk

Also available in this series

*Petbots: The Great Escape*
*Petbots: School Shutdown*

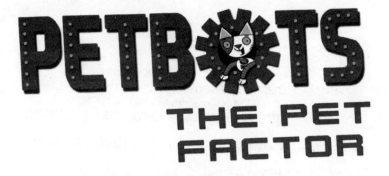

# PETB🐱TS
## THE PET FACTOR

### JUDY BROWN

Piccadilly
PRESS

First published in Great Britain in 2015
by Piccadilly Press
Northburgh House, 10 Northburgh Street, London EC1V 0AT
www.piccadillypress.co.uk

A CIP catalogue record for this book is available
from the British Library.

ISBN: 978–1–8481–2431–8

1 3 5 7 9 10 8 6 4 2

Typeset by Palimpsest Book Production Limited, Falkirk, Stirlingshire

Printed in the UK by Clays Ltd, St Ives plc

Piccadilly Press is an imprint of the Bonnier Publishing Group
www.bonnierpublishing.com

*Dedicated to*

*AB*

*for the music*

# Chapter 1

# Pet Factor Fever

*Crash! Clatter! Clang!*

Archie woke with a start to the sound of Flo crashing in a heap to the floor.

'What on earth are you doing, Flo?' he asked. 'You'll go through the classroom ceiling if you're not careful!'

Flo dusted herself off and flew back up to the beam she'd been balancing on.

'I'm practising pirouettes. I've been watching *Pet Factor* on the television,' she said. 'It's brilliant! All the children are talking about it.'

Archie the cat, Flo the bird and Sparky the mouse – the Petbots – were in their attic hideaway above the classrooms at Oakhill Primary School. Archie tuned in his radar ears to listen to the usual Monday-morning hubbub. It seemed that this morning the children were even more hyper than usual.

'I see what you mean, Flo,' said Archie. He played the conversation through his speakers so that they could all listen.

'I didn't think that *Pet Factor* would be as good as *X Factor* but it's amazing,' said one of the children.

'Some of those pets were really clever,' agreed another.

'Did you see those guinea pigs?' one of the Year Ones was saying. 'They were soooo fluffy! Couldn't you have just eaten them up?'

Sparky looked alarmed. Archie laughed.

'Don't worry, Sparky,' he said, 'it's just an expression.'

'What about the snake?' one of the other children said. 'That was scary.'

'I thought the best bit was the Chihuahua that danced a cha-cha.'

'No, the best bit was definitely that other dog that pooped on stage,' laughed someone else. 'Its owner was so embarrassed. That was awesome!'

There was lots of excited giggling, and Archie switched off his speakers.

The excitement had clearly spread to Sparky as well and he was whizzing at top speed around the attic, sparks flying.

'Would speed be my special talent?' he asked, darting in and out of the rafters.

'It's hard to think of another pet that could go faster than you, Sparky,' said Flo. 'That speed of yours has helped us out of trouble more than once.'

Archie looked puzzled. 'What's this *Pet Factor* all about then, Flo?'

Flo powered up the laptop and typed 'Pet Factor' into the search box. The *Pet Factor* website came up.

'People take along their talented pets and they perform in front of some judges. If they get

5

enough "yes" votes their pet gets through to the next round. You can watch video clips of some of the acts.' Flo clicked on one of a particularly perky-looking parrot.

Sparky zipped over to join them.

'Cor! Who knew they made bikes that small? Let's look at another one, Flo! What can that rabbit do?'

'I like this one,' said Flo. She clicked on a picture of a Chihuahua wearing a Mexican costume. 'Isn't he adorable? Look he dances the cha-cha with Carmelita, the lady with the massive blonde hairdo. That just has to be a wig.'

'It all looks a bit daft to me,' said Archie. 'I don't think I'd fancy getting up on a stage and performing like that.'

'But you're not an ordinary pet, are you, Archie? Anyway, it wouldn't be fair if you entered.' Flo imagined she was a contestant, performing in front of adoring fans. She did  a few more pirouettes, got a bit dizzy and fell over. It wasn't as easy as it looked.

Down in the 5B classroom, Mrs Kinsey was trying to get the lesson started as the last few stragglers arrived. Jack, Anya and Sophie were the Petbots' friends, and they were the only ones who knew that Archie, Flo and Sparky were living in the school attic.

'Did you watch *Pet Factor* on Saturday?' asked Anya. 'Everyone's talking about it.'

'Sure did,' said Jack. 'It was awesome, especially the show-jumping rabbits. My cousin's got rabbits and they're really boring. Too fat to do anything, and they just sit twitching their noses all day and stuffing their faces with carrots.'

'I liked the ducks,' added Sophie. 'How on earth did they get them to quack in time with the music?'

'Enough chatter, 5B,' said Mrs Kinsey. 'The sooner we get the register done, the sooner I can tell you some exciting news.'

A murmur of anticipation spread through the class.

Up in the attic, the Petbots were still sitting around the laptop watching video clips of the contestants. Some of them were brilliant, some were rather silly and some were just plain dreadful.

'Ha ha ha!' roared Archie. 'Have you ever heard anything so awful in your life?' he said as they watched a clip of a 'singing' dog.

'Shhhh, Archie!' warned Flo. 'It's quiet down there, they'll hear you!'

Archie clapped a metal paw over his mouth to stifle his giggles.

It was so quiet in 5B's classroom that the register was done in double-quick time.

'Well, class, I know how all of you have been enjoying watching *Pet Factor* over the last week,' Mrs Kinsey said. There were murmurs of agreement and a few spontaneous rounds of applause. 'Well, I'm thrilled to tell you that the auditions will be coming to our local theatre this week!' The whole class gasped. 'And that's not all,' she went on. 'The producers of the show have asked local schools to make an announcement that they are looking for new talent. The auditions will be happening all week long, so if you or anyone you

know has a pet they'd like to put forward for the
*Pet Factor*, now's your chance!'

Loud cheers filled the room.

# Chapter 2

# Excursion Plans

Jack, Anya and Sophie couldn't wait to see the Petbots at morning break. The children and the Petbots always met up on a Monday morning to catch up on any exciting news. The children sneaked into the stationery cupboard, their usual meeting place, eager to share the *Pet Factor* news.

Archie and the others saw them heading for the cupboard on their surveillance monitors and were ready and waiting when the children arrived. Archie and the others had installed the system of cameras and motion sensors to avoid being caught unawares by the nosey, grumpy old caretaker, Albert Sparrowhawk, who was always on the prowl.

'Did you hear?' said Anya. 'About *Pet Factor*, and the auditions?'

'Yes we did!' said Flo, flapping her metal wings excitedly. 'We've just been watching clips on the website.'

'This is the last week of auditions,' said Anya, 'and anyone who gets through now will be entered into the semi-final live on TV on Saturday! The public will vote for the winners and they'll go through to the live grand final in London a week later!'

'We're trying to persuade Sophie to take her cat Charlie to the audition,' said Jack.

'Oh! Why? What can he do?' Flo was beside herself.

'He's just a big old moggy,' Sophie explained, 'but he loves to sit at the piano and put his paws on the keys, especially when I'm doing my piano practice.'

'It's hilarious!' said Jack.

'You should get him a little bow tie, like soloists wear,' said Anya. 'He'd look so cute!'

'I wish I could come to the auditions,' said Flo.

'You should totally come!' said Jack. 'Nobody would notice you amongst all those animals.'

'And if Sophie's taking Charlie, you could come with us,' said Anya.

'Oh please, please, please can we? Can we?' Flo and Sparky pleaded.

Archie was quite intrigued by the whole thing, but he felt someone had to be sensible about it. The Professor had always warned him about the danger of discovery. When the Professor had built the Petbots he'd made sure to tell them that because they were such an amazing piece of robot engineering, if they fell into the wrong hands they might be dismantled to see how they worked and never put together again.

'I'll think about it,' Archie told them.

Flo, Sparky and the children huddled together in excitement.

*Bbrrinnggg!*

'There's the bell,' said Sophie. 'Back to class.'

'See you back here later!' Jack said.

As the Petbots went
back to the attic, Flo
was chattering away
about how much fun
the auditions would be.

'Don't get too
carried away,' said
Archie. He didn't want
Flo to be disappointed
if it wasn't possible to go. 'Let's find out exactly
where the auditions are going to be held.'

The Petbots gathered around the laptop.

'Okay, here's the map,' said Archie. 'It looks
like the theatre's actually not that far from here,
only about five minutes' flying time for you, Flo.'
She and Sparky looked at each other and grinned.
'Getting there wouldn't be a problem for Sparky

either,' Archie went on, 'because he can travel in someone's pocket.'

'But what about you, Archie?' asked Flo. 'We couldn't leave you behind.' Suddenly she looked a bit worried.

'Exactly. How can I get from here to there without being seen?'

Later on that day the children came back to the stationery cupboard, eager to find out whether the Petbots could come to the *Pet Factor* audition.

'Well?' Sophie asked anxiously.

Archie explained the problem.

'You could wear a disguise to get there, like you have before – you know, when you impersonated Mr Sparrowhawk and imitated his voice with your digital sampler,' Jack suggested.

'Yes, but it's too far for me to walk on two legs instead of four,' Archie told him.

'How about a pushchair?' asked Anya.

'I'm too big,' said Archie.

'Hang on . . .' Jack said. 'Do you remember last year when Robbie fell out of a tree and broke his leg?'

'Yes,' chorused Anya and Sophie.

'And we had to push him around everywhere in a wheelchair?'

Sophie smiled. 'I see where you're going with this.'

20

'I know for a fact that wheelchair is still in the sickroom.'

'We could borrow it . . .' said Anya. 'It might be hard work pushing it, though, Archie being so heavy.'

'Not if I powered it myself,' said Archie, an idea forming in his processors. 'I can rig up a motor to attach to the wheels and plug it into my powerpack. It shouldn't use up any more energy than if I was walking there, so it wouldn't run my batteries down.'

'Brilliant!' said Jack.

'All we have to do is think of a way to make a fake plaster cast for my leg,' Archie mused. 'It looks like we're coming with you after all!'

Sparky whizzed around doing celebratory wheelies. Then Flo tried to do a loop-the-loop

and ended up knocking a box of drawing pins off the top shelf! But Archie calmly stretched out a magnetised paw to pick them up and Sparky collected the pins that had rolled under the shelves. By the time he finished he looked a bit like a multicoloured hedgehog!

'Tomorrow's auditions start at five,' said Jack, 'but the doors open at four, so we'll meet you after school with the wheelchair.'

'Sparky and I will wait for you near the bicycle shed,' confirmed Archie.

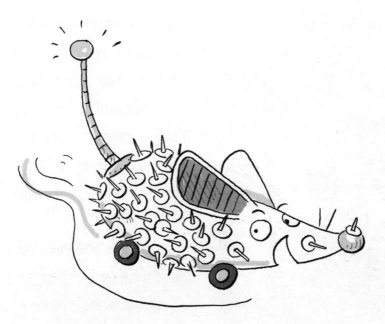

'Yay! We're going on an adventure!' twittered
Flo.

With that, the Petbots returned to the attic to
plan their route and the children went to afternoon
lessons. They were far too excited to concentrate.

## Chapter 3

# Audition Time!

Sophie, Jack and Anya were excited about *Pet Factor* but Sophie was also rather nervous. She and her mum were taking her cat Charlie along to audition!

'I hope he doesn't go all shy on me,' explained Sophie. 'Mum said I'll need to go on stage and play the piano with him, or he won't do it. I'll feel a real idiot if he just sits there and does nothing.'

'It'll be fine,' Anya assured her. 'Charlie's a natural performer.'

A few of the other children in the school were taking their pets to the audition too and it seemed to be the only topic of conversation in school. The day dragged on slowly. 5B's last lesson was PE and during football training Jack gave a performance worthy of an Oscar.

'Oooo! Oww! My ankle!' he wailed, after being tackled by another boy in the class.

'I never touched him, Miss!' said the boy indignantly.

'Oh dear,' said Mrs Kinsey, examining his leg. 'I can't see anything broken or swollen – can you walk?'

Jack 'tried' to stand.

'Ow, ow, ow!' he groaned.

Mrs Kinsey winced. 'We'd better get the office to ring your parents so they can come and pick you up.'

'Er,' said Jack quickly, 'our car's broken, Mrs Kinsey.'

Right on cue, Sophie piped up suddenly as if she'd just had a brilliant idea.

'I could take him home in the wheelchair from the sickroom,' she suggested helpfully. 'Jack only lives five minutes away from me.'

'How kind, Sophie,' said Mrs Kinsey, impressed with Sophie's generous offer. 'Do you think that will be okay, Jack?'

'I think it's just badly twisted, Miss. It will be fine if I don't walk on it.'

'I'll go and let the office know then,' she said. 'Everybody else back to the changing room. Anya, perhaps you can give Sophie a hand?'

Mrs Kinsey turned to go and when she was out of earshot, Jack, Sophie and Anya exchanged high fives.

When the bell finally rang, the school emptied

even more quickly than on the last day of term. Everyone was so excited about the *Pet Factor* audition!

The Petbots watched from the attic and laughed when they saw Sophie and Anya wheeling Jack through the gate, as if they were heading for home. Archie put on his disguise so he was ready to meet Jack and Anya by the bicycle shed. He was wearing a hooded top and jogging bottoms he'd found in the Lost Property box, and he extended his robotic legs, arms and neck to make himself taller so that the clothes would fit. Flo flew out of the attic window and  perched on the roof to keep a lookout for teachers.

'No one around!' she twittered cheerfully on their internal communication system. The intercom was how the Petbots communicated when they were out of earshot. Archie checked the surveillance monitors just to make sure. The headteacher was in his office, deeply engrossed in a game of Sweetie Slush Saga on his Facebook page and was oblivious to anything but the fruity 'pings'. Mr Sparrowhawk was the only other staff member still in the building, and he was in the basement setting mousetraps for the night.

'I don't understand it, I don't know why I never catch anything,' he grumbled to himself. 'They must be the cleverest mice on the planet. Every night they set these things off, but I never catch even one of the blighters.'

Sparky knew the reason for that.

'Okay, coast is clear,' said Archie. They sneaked out of the stationery cupboard, down the stairs and out of the school.

Anya was waiting on the other side of the fence near the bicycle shed with the wheelchair, as instructed, and Flo had flown down to join her. Sophie had gone home to collect her cat and Jack was just walking up the road towards them.

A very bouncy, crazy-looking puppy was with him too.

The closer that Archie got, the bouncier the puppy became. By the time Archie had reached them, it could no longer contain itself. It was clearly keen to make friends and circled round and round the Petbots, sniffing madly. Then he licked Archie's face . . . all over.

'Buster! Stop it!' cried Jack. 'Archie, this is my puppy, Buster. I decided to bring him to the audition!'

'But what can he do?' asked Anya. 'I've seen him with your mum and dad in the park – he's just mental.'

'Yeah, he is a bit,' Jack laughed, 'but he does sing along when he hears me singing. Well, howls really.'

'I'm not surprised,' said Anya. 'Your sing-ing's enough to make anyone howl!'

'Erm, hello, Buster, nice to

meet you I'm sure,' blurted
Archie through the licks,
'but if you could just calm
down . . .'

The others thought it
was hilarious.

Jack giggled. 'I think he
likes you.'

Flo nearly fell off the
fence laughing.

'Yes, and I like him too, but if you could get him
off me before his slobber gives me a short circuit,
I'd really appreciate it.'

'Come on, Buster,' said Jack, pulling the puppy
away, 'leave Archie alone.' Anya patted Buster's
head and he looked at her adoringly.

Archie took a plaster cast and a small electric

motor out of the bag he was carrying. He attached the motor to the back axle of the wheelchair and sat down. He closed the plaster cast over his leg. And put on a baseball cap.

'I love the plaster cast!' said Anya. 'Very convincing.'

'Thanks,' said Archie. 'We raided the art room last night. I hope nobody notices. Now, let's power this up.' He opened a small panel on his belly and plugged the motor into a power socket. There was a quiet 'hum' as the motor came to life. 'Here, Jack, this is for you. It's pretty obvious what you have to do.'

Jack looked at the control box that Archie had handed him. It had two buttons – one said 'start', one said 'stop'.

'I think even I can handle that!' he said.

'Just don't forget to steer,' added Archie. 'That's down to you.' Jack pressed 'start' and the wheelchair moved off smoothly.

Sparky zipped up and settled into Archie's lap.

'See you at the theatre, everybody!' said Flo and took to the sky.

Anya was right about how busy it was going to be. When they got to the theatre, there was quite a queue. The group could see Sophie and her mum near the front, though.

'Wow!' said Anya. 'You wouldn't think that there would be this many talented pets.'

Flo was perched on the roof of the theatre. When she saw Archie and the children arrive, she realised that she was probably just within range of Archie's intercom.

'Hi, Archie, can you hear me?' she asked.

'Loud and clear,' Archie answered. 'You made it okay, then?'

'Easy-peasy!' said Flo. 'I'm going inside now.'

'Take care,' Archie told her. 'And keep out of sight.'

'I intend to,' she replied. 'Over and out.'

Flo flew around the top floor of the building, looking for a sensible way in. She spotted a little window and prised it open with her powered beak and hopped inside.

'Great! No one around,' she said to herself and flew down the hallway. She found herself at the very top of the theatre, above the stage. 'Perfect! Bird's-eye view.' She flew over, found the best place to perch, and settled down on the lighting rig.

Back in the queue, it occurred to Jack that he hadn't really prepared Buster's 'act'. He had been rather caught up in the excitement of it all.

'I thought you said he was going to sing,' said Anya.

'Yes, but he won't sing unless I do and I didn't bring anything to sing along to,' Jack complained. 'Anya, I don't suppose that you'd . . .'

'Oh, no you don't, you're not getting me up on the stage, I wouldn't do it even if you paid me!' she warned him.

Jack began to feel a little sick. As usual, he

hadn't really thought things through.

'But I can't sing,' he said glumly.

'I'm sure there's something you can sing,' said Anya. 'Anyway, as long as we get in, that's what matters.

They were right at the front of the queue now and Jack was wishing he'd come up with a completely different plan. One that didn't involve Buster.

'Next please!' bellowed an incredibly cheery lady at the registration desk. Anya stood to one side with Archie in the wheelchair while Jack handed in his application. 'And who do we have here?' said the lady, who was wearing a badge that said 'Mindy'.

'This is Buster and I'm Jack.'

'And what is Buster going to do for us today, Jack?'

'Er, he's going to sing.'

'Sing!' exclaimed Mindy. 'What a clever-wevver little doggy.'

Archie wondered if she was speaking some strange language that the Professor hadn't included in his database. . . He'd never heard the word 'wevver' in his life.

'Well, here's your number. Aren't you just a wuvvley bundle of fluffy woof-woof?' said Mindy.

Archie began to think she was deranged.

'Aw, look at his ickle-wickle face.' She handed Jack a large piece of paper with '52' printed on it and noticed Anya standing nearby with Archie and his 'broken' leg. 'Oh dear, you've been in the wars, haven't you? Whatever happened, you poor little sausage?'

'Er, yes,' said Archie using his digital sampler to imitate Jack's voice, but pitching it slightly higher to sound younger, 'I hurt it playing football,' which was sort of true in a very roundabout way.

'Aww, blesss 'ooo!' Mindy said, but then she started to look at him a little too closely.

Archie shrank down into his hoody and pulled his cap down lower.

'He's a bit shy,' said Jack, grabbing the number.

'Bless his little cotton socks,' said Mindy. 'Follow the signs to the main auditorium where you can find somewhere to sit. Best of luck, my lovelies. Next please!'

## Chapter 4

# Charlie's Debut

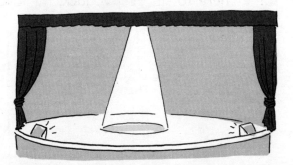

Anya peeked into the main auditorium. It was full of a strange assortment of pets of all shapes and sizes. She could see Sophie and her mum but they were clearly engrossed in getting their extremely large black-and-white cat Charlie ready for the audition, brushing him all over.

'It's pretty packed in there,' said Anya. 'I'm not

sure it's the place for an excitable Buster. Maybe we should go upstairs where it's quieter?'

They wheeled Archie over to the lift and pressed the button for the first floor. When the doors opened upstairs, Jack and Anya wheeled Archie down the aisle to where the balcony overlooked the stage. There were only a few people dotted about upstairs and they made themselves comfortable next to a short row of four seats right at the front.

'Are you there, Flo?' Archie asked through their intercom.

'Archie! You're in!' she scanned the theatre below and spotted them instantly. 'Hi, Sparky. I'm up here,' she said, 'in the lighting rig.'

Archie zoomed in on her and raised a metal paw in greeting. Sparky bounced up and down happily on the ledge of the balcony.

Archie looked down and saw that in front of the stage was a big desk with four judges sitting in a row. They each had a star that could light up in front of them, and over the stage were four 'yes' and 'no' lights. He wondered what they would make of Charlie . . . and Buster.

A stage manager called out, 'Number fifteen, can we have number fifteen on stage, please?'

A teenage boy with long hair and dressed all in black like a Goth, skateboarded slowly onto the stage. He had another, smaller skateboard under one arm and was followed by a scruffy little dog.

'Welcome, welcome!' said the presenter, who

introduced himself as Phil. Phil was part of the reason the show was so popular, but he'd never presented an animal version of this show before and he wasn't sure he would want to again. There had been some rather unpleasant smells to deal with and he'd found that the animals and their owners could be completely unpredictable – not always in a good way. 'Who are you and who have you brought with you?'

'Hi, I'm Damien and this is my dog, Dracula.'

Archie giggled. 'That's probably the least vampire-like dog I've ever seen.'

'And what does

Dracula do?' asked Phil. It seemed like a silly question to ask.

Damien leant into the microphone and said, 'He can skateboard.'

The audience of fellow pet owners and their friends clapped and cheered and the row of judges look impressed.

'Well, Damien and Dracula,' said Phil, 'off you go!'

Some heavy metal music started to play and Damien slowly skateboarded around the stage as Dracula sat and watched. Then Damien placed the small skateboard on the stage and Dracula climbed on it.

Damien had a lead attached to the front of Dracula's skateboard to help steer it around the stage. He skated and pulled Dracula along. It all went quite well to begin with and the audience cheered loudly.

'He's really good,' said Jack, worrying about how not-good he and Buster were likely to be.

'I'm impressed,' said Archie. 'He's not bad at all.'

Sparky, forgetting where he was, went

backwards and forwards along the balcony until Archie put a gentle paw on top of him to make him stay put, before someone noticed that there was a small metal mouse whizzing around.

The applause, however, began to go to Damien's head and he started to go faster and faster. Too fast, in fact. The lead got tangled in the wheels of his skateboard, and Dracula went

flying off his skateboard into the audience, narrowly missing one of the judges, who ducked just in time.

Poor Damien looked quite dejected when he didn't go through to the live TV show on Saturday, but the judges kindly suggested that he should practise more and try again next year.

Next up was a group of performing pigeons. Flo was thrilled.

'Hey, Archie, they look like me!' she said. 'But with real feathers, not metal ones.'

The act was a pigeon circus! Four of them rode on a roundabout, another two went on a swing boat, which they powered by pulling a string. But the best bit as far as Flo was concerned was the tightrope-walker pigeon, which did pirouettes on one leg all along the wire.

'Awesome,' she said.

Needless to say, the pigeon circus got four yeses from the judges. As the birds and their owner came off the stage, a little old lady with a clipboard approached them and chatted with the owner for a while, asking him questions and filling in a form.

The pigeon circus was followed by a footballing

pig, which dribbled a ball into a special little goal. Then came two performing goats that jumped through hoops and walked on barrels.

Flo and Sparky were thoroughly enjoying themselves, as was Archie.

'I must admit,' Archie said, 'it's even better than I thought it would be. I wonder when Sophie and Charlie will be on.'

'I'll go and find out,' said Anya. She ran off and reappeared downstairs, weaving her way through the people and pets to where Sophie and her mum were. Jack saw her pointing up at them and she held up her number – 23.

'We're on number twenty at the moment,' said Jack, who was watching another performing dog. This one could balance things on its nose – it wasn't making him feel any better about auditioning with Buster. 'Only two more and then it's Sophie! I bet she's nervous,' he said sympathetically, feeling butterflies in his own stomach.

As if she could hear what he'd said, Sophie mimed biting her nails when he waved and showed her his number. Jack mimed a fainting fit in reply, which made the girls laugh.

Anya came back upstairs, just as the following act, a monkey who could paint, was being dragged off the stage, rejected by the judges, having gone a bit wild with his paintbrush. Act 22, the one before Sophie and Charlie, was a troupe of performing mice.

Sparky, as you could imagine, was fascinated by this and sat almost motionless, except for his twitching whiskers, as he watched the display of basketball-playing, ball-balancing, flag-raising mice.

'I hope you're not getting any wild ideas about doing this at home,' said Archie, knowing that's exactly what Sparky was planning.

Sophie and Charlie were waiting in the wings when their number was called. Charlie, calmness personified until now, had spotted the bright lights of the stage and decided not to budge any further.

Sophie tugged at the lead attached to his collar. 'Come on, Charlie,' she pleaded, 'it's our turn.'

He looked up at her unimpressed and unmoved.

'Contestant number twenty-three,' said Phil, 'please join us on stage.'

Sophie tugged again. Charlie dug his claws in.

There was nothing for it, so Sophie picked up

the big lump of a cat and walked unsteadily
onto the stage, hoping that once they were
sitting at the piano he'd be more co-operative
than he was being now.

'Welcome, young lady, who are you and who
do we have here?'

'I'm Sophie,' said Sophie, 'and this is my cat,
Charlie. He plays piano.' There was a huge cheer

and a murmur of anticipation from the audience. The loudest cheers came from Anya, Jack and the Petbots. Sparky span excitedly in a circle.

'Good luck,' whispered Flo, crossing her feathers.

Charlie was certainly a big cat and his fluffy coat made him look even bigger. It was a relief when Sophie could put him down on the piano stool next to her. Then she began to play. She'd thought a lot about what tune she should play and had decided on something easy so that she didn't make any mistakes. 'Three Blind Mice' seemed appropriate – her only worry was that Charlie wouldn't play along. But Charlie was a natural: Sophie had barely got to 'see how they run' and Charlie had started pressing keys.

The audience loved it, clapping and cheering enthusiastically.

'Well done, Charlie!' shouted Archie.

Charlie seemed spurred on by the cheering and stood on the piano with all four paws to play more notes. The cheering got louder.

'They love it!' cheered Anya. She felt really proud of Sophie and Charlie. She almost began to get teary.

Then Charlie walked up and down the keyboard

as Sophie carried on playing the tune. The place was in uproar.

'Hooray!' shouted Jack. 'More! More!'

The judges were all thrilled and four green 'YES' votes lit up. Charlie and Sophie were through to the live semi-final on Saturday!

## Chapter 5

# Funny Farm

'Way to go, Sophie!' said Jack. He and Anya did a high five.

'And Charlie!' said Archie.

'Of course,' said Anya. 'What a team. I think they've really got a chance.'

Above the stage, Flo was flapping her wings so excitedly that she nearly fell off her perch.

Sophie gathered Charlie up in her arms and walked off the stage with him, beaming happily. The little old lady with the clipboard approached her.

'That was marvellous, dear,' she said, 'you must be so proud.'

'Thank you,' said Sophie politely and cuddled Charlie, who nuzzled her back.

'I just need to take a few details,' the lady went on. 'What's your address, dear, are you local?'

'My mum already filled in an audition form, I think,' Sophie said.

'Ah yes, I know, dear,' she said, going to stroke Charlie's head but he backed away nervously and swiped at her with his paw, 'this is for our local newsletter, and maybe even the newspaper.'

'Oh, okay!' said Sophie, feeling important.

When the lady had asked her a few more questions, Sophie went back to her seat where her mum was waiting. Anya had run down to join them and there were hugs all round.

'Come and see Jack and Ar— er . . . Buster,' said Anya. 'They're upstairs.'

'Is it okay, Mum?' asked Sophie.

'Yes, of course,' said her mum, 'but then I think

we'd better be off, Charlie's probably had enough for one day.' Sure enough, their big old cat had crawled back into the pet carrier and fallen fast asleep.

Charlie wasn't the only one asleep. Buster was worn out by all the excitement and was having a puppy nap, wagging his tail in his sleep.

'He doesn't look much like he wants to go on stage,' laughed Sophie.

'I know! Not like you, Sophie. You and Charlie were awesome,' said Jack. He was beginning to feel physically sick at the idea of performing.

'Thank you,' said Sophie, blushing slightly. 'It was all Charlie, really.'

Sparky whizzed up and perched on her shoulder.

'Did you like it, Archie?'

'It was very good, but maybe you should teach him to play proper notes,' Archie said helpfully.

'I tried that once but he just got bored. What

 are you and Buster going to sing, Jack?' Sophie asked.

'I have no idea,' he said, turning a little green. 'What number are we up to now?'

'This is number forty,' Archie replied. 'More performing pooches.' He was beginning to get a little bored.

They carried on watching for a while, but when contestant number forty-eight came onto the stage, Jack was experiencing a fairly severe case of stage fright.

'Time to get ready,' said Anya. She gave Buster a nudge. He was still sound asleep.

'I don't think I can do it!' said Jack, a look of blind panic on his face. Anya only needed to take one look at him to see he was deadly serious.

'It's okay,' she said sympathetically. 'We'll tell them you're ill or something. Are you sure you don't want to go on?'

'Positive!' Jack had never been so sure of anything in his life! 'Come *on*, Buster,' said Jack, anxious to get going.

Buster yawned and stretched.

'Where am I?' he thought sleepily, then he remembered and got all excited. He jumped around the seats, full of energy. Jack grabbed his lead and dragged him over to the stairs.

'Flo,' said Archie, 'we're off. Jack and Buster aren't ready for their stage debut. Are you coming?'

'I'll stay and watch a bit more if that's okay,' said Flo. 'I know the way back.'

'Okay, see you back at home,' said Archie.

Unfortunately, Jack had underestimated how long it would take to get the wheelchair back downstairs and out of the building. First they had to wait for the lift to come back up, and then there was a queue of people and pets waiting to use it. By the time everybody in front had climbed in, there was barely room for them.

'Excuse us!' said Jack, as he squeezed the chair inside.

'Ow! That's my foot!' said a lady who was taking up half of the lift with her pet ostrich.

'So sorry,' apologised Jack, ducking just in time as the ostrich went to peck him.

As the lift descended, Jack could hear that they were calling his number and he was still holding it in one hand as the doors of the lift opened and the passengers, packed in like sardines, practically fell out. One of the assistants came out of the doors from the auditorium.

'Number fifty-two, calling number fifty-two.'

Jack opened his mouth to make his excuses, but it was too late.

'Ah! There you are,' said the assistant. 'You nearly missed your turn.'

So Jack and Buster – who was full of energy now – were ushered towards the auditorium.

'But I don't . . .' Jack tried to say.

'Come along, it's Buster the singing dog, isn't it?'

They were bustled through the door and down to the stage, Jack protesting all the way.

'But we're not ready . . . I don't feel well . . . er . . . Buster needs more practise . . .'

'Nonsense, it's just nerves,' said the assistant.
Before he knew it Jack was on stage.

Anya looked through a crack in the door.

'Oh dear,' she said.

Up in the lighting rig, Flo was surprised to say
the least.

'Are you still here, Archie? What's going on?' she asked over their intercom. 'Jack's just come on stage.'

'I'll explain later, Flo,' said Archie. 'Wish him luck. He's going to need it.'

'Welcome, welcome!' said Phil the presenter, a little less enthusiastically than earlier. 'What are your names?'

Staring at all the faces staring up at him, Jack was struck dumb with terror.

'It's Jack and Buster, isn't it?' said Phil, realising Jack needed some help. 'And what can Buster do?' he asked.

'Buster sings – well, howls really,' said Jack, blushing like a beetroot.

'Oh, right . . .' said Phil, obviously unimpressed. 'Well, take it away, Jack and Buster.'

Jack took a leaf out of Sophie's book and went for the simplest song he could think of.

'He-hem.' Jack cleared his throat, took a deep breath and began. 'Old MacDonald had a farm, E-I-E-I-O . . .'

Now Jack's singing voice wasn't good at the best of times, and feeling nervous and standing in front of a theatre full of people really didn't help. Some of them discreetly put their fingers in their ears. A couple of toddlers started to cry.

Jack soldiered on, but what made things worse was that Buster didn't seem remotely interested in joining in. He was far more interested in smelling all the amazing new smells that the other animals had left on the stage.

People began to giggle. Flo could barely watch. By the time that Jack had gone through the cows, ducks and pigs that Old MacDonald had on his farm, nearly every other dog in the building was howling, but it was clear that Buster was having none of it. In fact, what he did next was far worse.

He trotted over to Phil the presenter, who was standing at the edge of the stage waiting to announce the next act, lifted his leg and peed. All over Phil's foot.

The audience erupted! The judges fell about

laughing. Jack was mortified when he realised that Phil was now standing in a puddle of Buster's wee. He ran over, scooped up the puppy and fled, just as four big red 'NO's lit up over the stage.

'That was the most embarrassing moment of my entire life,' said Jack as they walked back to the

school with Archie in the wheelchair and Sparky sitting on his lap. 'If someone uploads it to YouTube, I'm never leaving the house again.'

Anya tried to cheer him up by changing the subject.

'Archie, Flo and Sparky had a good time, though,' she said, 'didn't you, guys?'

'Yes!' Archie and Sparky said together.

'And Charlie was awesome,' Jack said, trying to forget his terrible audition.

Back at the theatre, things were winding down.

Flo, still perched high up on the lighting rig, was watching the last few contestants. She'd seen the little old lady with the clipboard talk to many pet owners, but not all of them. 'I wonder why?' Flo asked

herself. She also felt that she'd seen the lady before somewhere but couldn't work out where.

The judges left, the theatre emptied and Flo decided it was time to go home. She flew back to the window she'd opened earlier and climbed back out onto the roof. Then something odd was captured by her visual sensors. The little old lady

with the clipboard was getting into a battered old van in the car park. Flo used her telescopic vision to zoom in on the writing on the side of the van. It was faded and peeling in places but she could still read it.

'Peggy's Pet Emporium. That's strange,' thought Flo, as she headed home. So the old lady wasn't

part of the *Pet Factor* crew. I wonder what the clipboard was for?

Peggy was on her way home. On the seat next to her was a scrawny little Chihuahua wearing a massive blue bow.

'Well, Chico,' said Peggy, 'quite a few talented pets today and I have all of their details. It's going to be a busy evening.'

'Yip!' yapped Chico.

## Chapter 6

# Bad News

The next morning, Flo's mind was still buzzing with the excitement of the auditions, and the first thing she did when she got up was browse the *Pet Factor* website to see if there was any mention of Charlie. Instead she found some surprising news.

'Hey, Archie, look at this,' she said. 'Some of the

pets from last week's auditions which went through to the semi-finals, have been withdrawn from the competition. It says here that Dennis the Dancing Dachshund and Mia the Meerkat have been withdrawn by their owners on medical advice – what a shame.'

'They were two of the best ones,' said Sparky. 'Even more of a chance for Sophie and Charlie then.'

'Oooh, I hadn't thought of that!' said Flo. 'I can't wait to see her and tell her how well they did.'

News about Sophie's success had spread around the school pretty fast and she'd become a bit of a celebrity. Fortunately, only a few of them had heard about Jack's woeful performance, so all he'd had to deal with were a few nudges and giggles in the corridors.

As soon as the group met up in the stationery cupboard, Flo flew over and gave Sophie a big hug.

'Aw, thanks, Flo,' Sophie said.

'Did you hear about the acts that pulled out?' asked Jack. 'I reckon Charlie could win the whole competition.'

'I've got to get through Saturday's semi-final first,' said Sophie. 'It's going to be really scary doing it in on live TV.'

'You'll be brilliant,' said Flo. 'I know you will.'

'If it's live on TV we can watch it here,' said Archie.

'It's not the same,' grumbled Flo. 'Couldn't I go on my own to the theatre?'

'But what if something happened to you?' Archie said. 'The Professor made me promise to look after you and Sparky and if I wasn't with you and you got into trouble there'd be nothing I could do.'

Despite her disappointment, Flo understood. It was nice that Archie cared so much.

The Petbots didn't see the children for the rest of the day. Sophie was kept busy by the stream of children wanting to hear all about her audition. By the time school was finished she was exhausted!

When the building was empty, Sparky got busy down in the basement doing his usual round, setting off the mousetraps set by Sparrowhawk the caretaker. He did it every night, just in case there were any real mice down there who might get caught by the traps, although he'd never actually seen one. It was great for speed and agility training, and each night Sparky tried to

see how fast he could spring the traps. This evening, inspired by what he'd seen at the theatre, he beat his record time by a whole four seconds.

Flo decided to have yet another look on the *Pet Factor* website to see if there was any more news.

'Hey, Archie! Look at this,' she said. 'There's a special announcement.' Flo read out what was on the screen. 'News is emerging that four of the pets tipped for success in *Pet Factor*'s grand final have disappeared. Their owners have made no comments, but as many other competitors have

also withdrawn for a variety of reasons, the producers have asked anyone with relevant information to come forward. Saturday's live semi-final will go ahead as planned.'

'That's odd,' said Archie. 'Did you notice anything strange yesterday, Flo? You were there until the end and you had a bird's-eye view of the whole place.'

'Nothing especially unusual,' she said, thinking hard. Then she remembered the van. 'Although, there was that little old lady with the clipboard . . .'

## Chapter 7

# Worse News

The next day, on the other side of town, Peggy's Pet Emporium was opening for business a little later than usual. Peggy picked up the local newspaper that had just come through the door and chuckled when she saw the headline on the front page.

It was about the missing *Pet Factor* competitors.
She was still reading when a customer came
in.

'You're late to open this morning, Peggy.'

'Morning, Mrs Parkinson,' said Peggy. 'Yes,
sorry about that, things to sort out at home.'

'Terrible business, isn't it?' commented Mrs
Parkinson, pointing to the paper. 'It's a good job

your little Chico is safe.' She looked down at the skinny little Chihuahua dozing in his lavish basket – he was obviously spoilt rotten. 'I saw you both on the telly last week. Wasn't he a little star? And that costume he wore?! So adorable! We voted for him, didn't we, Mac?' Mac, her scruffy old Scottie dog, wagged his tail happily. 'Mind you, I hardly recognised you in your glamorous wig,

and I never knew your name was Carmelita, I thought it was Peggy.'

'It's my middle name, explained Peggy, 'and I like to look my best when I'm on stage, you know, Mrs P. The usual, is it?' Mrs Parkinson had been coming in once a week on a Thursday for the past fifteen years. For *one* dog chew each time.

'Yes, please. You must be excited about the live grand final!'

Peggy handed her the chew.

'Have this one on me, Mrs P,' answered Peggy. Her plan was going so well she was feeling generous.

'Oh, how kind. I really shouldn't,' said Mrs Parkinson, grabbing the bag before Peggy changed her mind. 'Mind you, if your Chico wins

the competition you'll be rolling in it! Toodlepip!'
she called, wheeling her shopping trolley out of
the shop.

Peggy looked at
Chico.

'With all the others
out of the way there'll
be no one to beat us,'
she said with a glint in
her eye. 'That snake's a
tricky blighter, though,
and the parrot is driving
me nuts. If I hear

"Supercalifragilisticexpialidocious" one more
time, I may have to throttle it. Never mind, at
least we can't hear them all when we're here at

the shop. Thank goodness I decided not to keep them in the back room. And once we've won *Pet Factor* I can get rid of them. I think I'll sell them all to foreign customers,' said Peggy with a cackle.

Chico opened one eye and looked up at her. He wasn't really asleep, he was trying to avoid the dance practice – and the costume. 'I hate that sombrero,' he grumbled to himself. 'Stupid thing hurts my ears.'

Peggy yawned. 'I need a coffee,' she said. 'It was such a busy night!'

When Sophie arrived at school, it was clear that something was wrong.

'Hi, Sophie,' said Jack. 'You look awful! Are you ill?'

'No, I'm just worried,' she said. 'Look what came through the letterbox this morning. It was hand-delivered.' She showed Jack and Anya the letter that had arrived in the night. It was made out of cut-out letters from magazines and newspapers. It read:

unless you withdraw
Charlie from the competition
He will be Petnapped!
You have Until
Saturday morNing.
If you tell anyone
About this LETTer
You will nEvEr SEE
Charlie Again!

P.S. this iS not a Joke...

'Oh, Sophie!' said Anya. 'No wonder you're worried.'

'I know it says "Don't tell anyone" but I knew I could trust you guys,' she said.

'You have to show this to Archie,' said Jack, 'he'll know what to do.'

'That's why I brought it to school,' said Sophie sadly. 'The Petbots are the only ones who can help!'

Back at Peggy's Pet Emporium, the cup of coffee had filled Peggy with energy.

Chico the Chihuahua looked up at her wistfully, knowing exactly what was coming next. Peggy turned on the CD player and a Mexican cha-cha filled the shop.

She took a Mexican-style dog coat out of the drawer and fastened it on Chico, put a tiny sombrero on his head and then started to dance around the room.

Chico sighed. 'Here we go again,' he thought.

'Come on, Chico, it's time to cha-cha!'

# Chapter 8

# Peggy's Pet Emporium

'This is really serious,' said Archie, after reading Sophie's letter. 'Are you sure you shouldn't tell the police?'

'Look what it says,' she replied. '"Don't tell anyone." If I do, whoever it is might take Charlie and not give him back and it would all be my fault.'

Flo put a comforting wing round her shoulder. 'What can we do, Archie?' she asked.

Sparky was really angry. He whizzed around the cupboard, sparks flying everywhere. 'It makes me so mad,' he said. 'Those poor pets!'

'Steady, Sparky, you'll start a fire if you're not careful,' warned Archie.

Sparky slowed down and settled next to Sophie.

'We can't let them get away with this,' said Archie. 'My guess is it's one of the other contestants thinning out the competition.'

'To give themselves a better chance of winning?' asked Jack.

'Exactly,' said Flo.

'But what do you think they're doing with the animals?' said Anya. 'What's happening to them?'

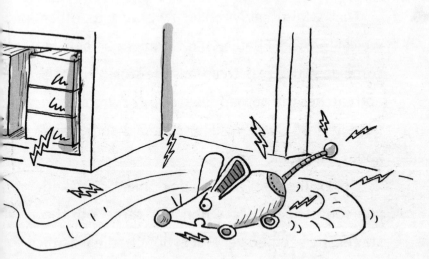

Archie looked serious. 'Hopefully they're being looked after and will be returned to their owners after the grand final.'

'There's nothing for it,' said Sophie. 'I'll just have to withdraw.'

'No, you have to perform! If Archie's right,' said Jack, 'the first people to investigate are the acts who are still in the competition.'

'That's right,' said Archie. 'If we work together we can protect Charlie. *And* we might be able to come up with a plan that finds the stolen animals and catches the petnapper in one go.' Archie was getting fired up now. 'Flo, you said something about a little old lady?'

'Oh, I remember her,' said Sophie. 'She asked me some questions when we came off the stage. She seemed very nice, but Charlie wasn't keen on her. It's funny, he usually loves a fuss.'

Archie frowned. 'What did she want to know, Sophie?'

'She asked me for my address and some other details – it was for a newsletter or the local paper, I think. She spoke with everyone who got through. To be honest I was still buzzing from Charlie's performance and all the applause, so I didn't take much notice.'

'She didn't talk to everyone,' corrected Flo. 'And I saw her drive away in this van, so I don't think she works for the newspaper . . .' Flo projected a piece of film from her memory banks onto the wall. It was Peggy getting into the van outside the theatre.

'"Peggy's Pet Emporium",' read Anya. 'That's the funny old pet shop near the station.'

'So you know where it is?' Archie said.

Anya nodded.

'Why don't we check it out after school?' suggested Jack.

'Good idea,' agreed Anya.

Archie was quiet and the light in his eyes was pulsing gently, which meant he was thinking hard about something.

'I have an idea!' he announced. 'What if I take Charlie's place on Saturday – what if I pretend to be him? Then I can investigate backstage, and if I'm petnapped, we can use our tracking system to  pinpoint the criminals *and* the pets!'

'You'd do that for me and Charlie?' asked Sophie, flinging her arms round him. 'That's so brave!'

'We pets have to stick together,' Archie said.

'So Archie would have to do Charlie's act – play the piano?' asked Anya.

Suddenly Archie wondered if it been such a good idea after all. He wasn't really used to going out in public, let alone performing on stage. Unsurprisingly, playing the piano hadn't been an ability the Professor thought necessary for a robot cat.

'I hate to point it out,' said Jack, 'but Archie doesn't exactly look a lot like Charlie. I think people are going to notice! He's much bigger, for one thing, and he hasn't got any fur.'

'Hmm,' said Archie. 'Well, I can make myself smaller by retracting my legs and arms so I'm Charlie's size, but I can't grow fur, I'm afraid.'

'We could make him a costume!' suggested Anya.

'Yes, yes! My mum's got all that white fur fabric left over from the polar bear costumes she made for the school play.'

'Whoa, whoa!' said Archie, holding up a paw.

'This is getting out of hand. I never agreed to dressing up.'

'But it's the only way you'd get away with it,' said Jack.

'They have a point, Archie,' Flo told him. 'The plan won't work unless you look like Charlie.'

Archie winced. It was something he'd rather overlooked. He really couldn't picture himself in a cat costume performing in a talent show. It seemed a little bit silly for a robot cat with his own particular digital talents. He sighed, then nodded his agreement.

'That's settled then,' said Sophie. 'Anya, you'll have to come over to my house tomorrow night and stay over so we can make the costume.'

'That means we'll need Archie at your house too, to make sure it fits properly.'

'Good point,' agreed Sophie. 'He'd have to be there on Saturday morning to leave for the competition anyway.'

'Ooooh, ooooh!' Flo said. 'A sleepover!' This is so exciting!'

Archie had a feeling things were getting out of control.

'Now wait,' he said. 'We can't just wander over to your house.'

'No,' said Sophie, 'but if Jack and Anya come round for tea, I'm sure Mum would come and pick us up – we could smuggle you into the boot or something.'

'Perfect!' said Flo, 'and I'll fly behind the car and follow you home.' If she had been any more excited, she would probably have exploded.

'Can I go in your pocket?' asked Sparky, happily doing wheelies around the cupboard again.

Sophie smiled. 'Of course you can.'

'We'll need power points to charge up overnight,' Archie pointed out.

'No problem,' she said, 'you can do that in my room.'

'It's going to be so great!' said Flo.

Archie hoped their plan was as simple as it sounded.

After school, Jack, Anya and Sophie walked home via Peggy's Pet Emporium.

'You two had better wait outside,' said Anya. 'If there is something fishy going on and she recognises you, she might get suspicious.'

'Fair enough,' said Sophie.

Anya pushed the door open. *Tinkle, tinkle* rang the bell over the door.

The shop was shabby and dingy, crammed with

stock that looked very old. It really needed a makeover. There were lots of newspaper articles displayed on the walls: some were about pet shows, others were stories about talented pets.  The sound of Mexican music playing quietly was coming from the back of the shop.

The owner, a short lady with grey hair, was on the phone. Anya recognised her from the film that Flo had shown them and realised this must be Peggy. She could see that Peggy had been reading about the missing pets in the local paper.

'Yes, I know, Mrs Brown, it's awful, isn't it? It's

all over the papers.' She paused, put her hand over the mouthpiece and spoke to Anya. 'Can I help you, dear?' she asked.

'Er, just browsing,' answered Anya, who was

happy to eavesdrop and take a look around the shop.

'Yes, dear, Chico's here safe with me, but who knows what's happened to those other poor animals? Anyway, I'd better go, I've a customer in the shop. Must go. Bye, dear.' Peggy put the

phone down. 'Were you looking for something in particular?' she asked Anya.

'Umm,' said Anya, aware of the fact that she only had twenty pence in her pocket. She scanned the shelves for something cheap and spotted a catnip mouse in the 'reduced' box. 'Just this!' she said triumphantly, walking over to the counter.

'Big spender', thought Peggy. 'And that's all, is it?'

'Yes, thank you. Terrible about those pets going missing, isn't it?' she replied, handing over her twenty pence. 'So do you have a pet in the competition yourself?' Anya asked casually. There was something really familiar about Peggy but Anya couldn't put her finger on it. She glanced past Peggy into the room behind the counter, noticed a big blonde wig on a stand and it suddenly dawned on her where she'd seen Peggy before.

'Er, yes, dear, that's right,' said Peggy, 'but with all this trouble, I'm not sure if I really want to carry on.' She put the catnip mouse into a paper bag. 'Here you are, dear, please come again.'

'Thank you,' said Anya. She smiled sweetly and left the shop.

Peggy stood quietly, thinking for a moment. She had an uneasy feeling about her young customer.

'What did you find out?' asked Jack as they walked away from the shop.

'Well,' said Anya. 'You'll never guess who Peggy is!'

'Who?' asked Jack.

'There was cha-cha music coming from the back room of the shop.'

'And?' Jack said.

'And then I saw a big blonde wig in the back room.'

'So what?'

'You remember Chico, the dancing dog in the first round?'

'Yes,' said Sophie, 'it was really cute.'

'Peggy is Carmelita, Chico's owner! We didn't recognise her yesterday without the massive wig.'

'So do you think she's a suspect?' asked Sophie.

'Dunno,' said Anya, 'she said she was thinking of pulling out because of all the trouble, and she could have written for the

121

local paper, I guess. There were loads of articles on the wall.'

'Nothing concrete then,' said Jack.

'Nope,' said Anya. 'But I wonder what she was doing at the auditions if she'd already got through.'

# Chapter 9

# The Sleepover

The Petbots spent the next day preparing to stay over at Sophie's house. Flo was ecstatic to be going for a sleepover.

'It's going to be brilliant!' she said. 'I can't wait to see Sophie's house.'

'Do you think she's got a garden?' asked Sparky.

'I don't know, but we'll have to stay out of

sight, in Sophie's room,' Archie reminded them.

'Yes, I know, I know,' said Flo.

'I've printed a list of tools to take in case we need any emergency repairs,' said Archie, always wanting to be well prepared. 'Do you two want to start getting it together? I'm going to do a bit of practice on how to behave more like a real cat.'

So while Sparky and Flo packed a tool kit, Archie watched some cat videos on the Internet. First of all he did some cat-like stretches – they actually felt rather good! Then he tried pretending he was rubbing against people's

legs using some boxes – but he knocked them over.

Flo chuckled.

'You're too strong, Archie!' she said. 'You have to do it gently.'

Next Archie practised meowing and purring, but he got a bit carried away.

Flo was watching 5B in the classroom below

on the monitors. They were having a lesson about Egyptian mummies, a particular favourite of hers. Suddenly she realised that they could hear Archie. They were all looking around for a cat.

'Shhhh, Archie!' said Flo. 'The Year Fives can hear you.'

'Oops. Sorry, Flo,' he whispered.

Below, Sophie, Jack and Anya had a fair idea where the sounds were coming from.

'Archie must be practising how to be a cat!' giggled Sophie. 'How adorable!'

When the group met up at lunchtime, Anya told Archie about their trip to the pet shop.

'Nothing solid to go on then,' said Archie.

'Not really,' she said, 'but I think Peggy the pet shop owner might have something to do with it. You'll never guess who she is . . . she's Carmelita, the lady with the dancing Chihuahua! She looks completely different without the wig.'

'Of course!' said Flo. 'I knew she looked familiar.'

'Interesting,' said Archie, 'so we'll definitely watch her carefully. Are we all set for later?'

'Yep,' said Jack. 'We'll meet you in the stationery cupboard at the end of school and smuggle you out. Sophie's mum is expecting us all for tea, and Anya is staying over.'

'We've got the fur fabric and we've borrowed some fabric paint from the art room for the black patches,' said Sophie. 'How's the cat practice going?'

Archie walked over and rubbed against their legs to demonstrate, then purred quietly.

'Excellent!' She stroked his head. 'All you need now is the fur.'

The rest of the day dragged for the children, but in the attic the Petbots were busy rehearsing. Flo was projecting Charlie's performance and Archie was copying him, using a paper keyboard that they printed out and stuck together. He'd even managed to have a go on the school piano overnight.

'You don't want to play *too* well, though, Archie,' said Flo. 'It would look suspicious.'

'I suppose so,' agreed Archie. 'I need to be good enough to attract the petnapper's attention, though. Which reminds me,' he said, picking up a small metal box, 'I've modelled this transmitter to send out a signal so that you can both track me. It's tuned into your operating systems.'

'Cool!' said Sparky. 'It's magnetic, so I'll attach it under my costume and activate it when we're ready.'

The bell rang for the end of school.

'Right,' said Archie, 'let's check the monitors to see when the coast is clear.'

Flo and Sparky were excited enough to burst. Fifteen minutes later, Anya came to the cupboard as arranged.

'Sophie and Jack are outside waiting for her

mum, and there's no one else around at the moment. Are you all ready?' asked Anya.

'All ready,' confirmed Archie. 'Flo, you'd better fly onto the roof and wait for us to come out.'

She didn't need to be told twice and went off in a flurry of metal feathers. Anya put Sparky in her pocket, and Archie picked up the portable repair kit.

When Sophie saw her mum's car turn into the road, she waved to Flo, who was perched on the roof waiting eagerly for her signal.

'Sophie's mum's here,' Flo told Archie and Sparky over their intercom.

'Hi, kids!' said Sophie's mum from the car window.

'Hi, Mum,' said Sophie. 'Anya's just coming. I'll put our stuff in the boot.'

Jack engaged Sophie's mum in conversation, while Anya, closely followed by Archie, exited the school and headed for the car.

'Are you excited about the live semi-final tomorrow, Mrs Stuart?' he asked, keeping half an eye on Anya and Archie. 'Charlie was awesome, wasn't he?'

'Quick!' whispered Sophie. 'Hop in, Archie!'

Archie got into the boot and the children moved the bags to cover him up.

'All done,' said Sophie, shutting the boot. She and Anya got into the back seat.

'Off we go then,' said Mrs Stuart.

Back at Sophie's house, her mum parked the car on the driveway.

'Do you need a hand with your stuff?' she asked.

'No, Mum, we're fine thanks,' said Sophie.

Her mum opened the front door and went inside the house.

'Quick!' said Jack. He opened the car boot and ushered Archie inside and up the stairs. Charlie was on the landing, yawning, stretching and wondering what all the sudden activity was about. When he saw Sophie he began scratching at her bedroom door.

'Not now, Charlie,' she said, tickling him under the chin, 'we've got things to do.'

The first thing they did when they entered Sophie's room was open the window. Flo fluttered in, landed on Sophie's bed and looked around.

'It's just how I thought it would be!' she said. 'It's very you.'

'Er, thank you, I think,' said Sophie.

'Right,' said Archie quietly, 'we'd better make a start. Sparky, do your stuff.'

'Okay, boss!' said Sparky. The smallest petbot whizzed round Archie using his laser vision to take accurate measurements of Archie's dimensions. Archie made sure he'd made himself exactly  the same size as the real cat. Flo, fascinated by Sophie's room, was investigating every corner of it. She especially liked the large mirror framed with fairy lights.

When Sparky had finished he transmitted the measurements to Archie, who converted them into a pattern for the costume, which he downloaded to the laptop. Then it was Flo's job to project the pattern onto the fur material ready for cutting. The children sat and watched in awe at the efficiency of the process.

'Perfect!' said Sophie. 'I'll fetch Mum's dressmaking scissors.'

Archie smiled. 'No need – Flo, over to you.'

Flo set to work with her powered beak and the pattern was cut out in no time.

'Brilliant!' cried Anya.

'The sewing is all up to you, I'm afraid,' said

Archie. 'We weren't programmed to deal with needles and thread.'

Sophie and Anya looked at each other.

'I'm rubbish at sewing,' complained Anya.

'Me too,' said Sophie.

'Don't look at me,' said Jack, holding his hands up in surrender. 'Anyway, I have to leave after tea.'

'We'll manage somehow,' Sophie assured them.

'How hard can it be?' said Archie.

After tea Jack dashed back upstairs to say goodbye to the Petbots as Anya and Sophie helped in the kitchen.

'See you at the competition tomorrow,' he said. 'I can't wait to see how the costume turns out!'

Archie raised an eyebrow.

The sewing did not go well. By the time the girls had sewn all the pieces together there were far more lumps and bumps than there should have been. They put the costume on Archie to see how it fitted.

Archie looked in the mirror. He could see that Flo, Sparky, Sophie and Anya were trying desperately not to laugh. It was obvious why – he looked ridiculous.

'This is humiliating,' he said.

Flo was giggling. 'It's not that bad. It's just a bit, er, *baggy* here and there.'

'Yes,' said Sophie, 'but the black splodges will help loads. I'll get Charlie so that we can get the shapes right.'

She opened the door to find Charlie sitting patiently outside. He strolled in and stopped dead when he saw the strange-looking cat in Sophie's room. Sparky quickly hid under the bed in case Charlie was the kind of cat that liked chasing mice. Fortunately, Charlie was very easy-going and rather than hissing and spitting he stalked over to give Archie a sniff. It gave the girls the perfect opportunity to paint black patches onto Archie's costume to match Charlie's fur.

'There!' Sophie stepped back to admire their handiwork. Sparky, forgetting his earlier caution, zipped around the room to get a view from every angle. Charlie spotted him and tried to pounce, but Sparky was much too fast. After a couple of half-hearted swipes with his paw Charlie gave up and wandered towards Sophie's door to head downstairs for food.

With the black patches painted on, the costume looked a whole lot better and Archie felt a little less stupid.

'You look amazing!' said Flo.

'Cool!' Sparky agreed.

Archie did a couple of circuits of the room, practising his cat moves. It was hilarious!

'I never knew you were such a good actor!' Anya had tears rolling down her face. Sophie couldn't speak she was laughing so much.

'He's been practising all day,' said Flo proudly.

After they'd cleared up all the mess they'd made, and started to get ready for bed, Sophie suddenly had a worrying thought.

'We have to take you in the pet carrier, don't we?'

'Yes,' replied Archie. 'Why?'

'Well, I won't be able to carry you in it. You're too heavy.'

'She's right, you know,' said Flo.

Archie thought for a moment.

'Can you bring the carrier here?' he asked. He knew what to do.

Sophie went downstairs and returned with the carrier almost immediately.

'Sparky,' said Archie, 'can you use your laser to make four holes in the bottom? If that's okay, Sophie?'

'Um, what for?' she asked, puzzled.

Archie held up a metal paw and pointed to the underside of the carrier.

'Your wheels!' exclaimed Anya.

'One of the extra attachments the Prof thought

of. If the carrier is close enough to the ground you can wheel me along.'

'Great idea,' said Sophie. 'Go for it, Sparky.'

When Sparky had finished, Sophie put Charlie's blanket back inside the carrier so her mum didn't see the holes. Afterwards, tired out from all the hard work, they all settled down for the night. Archie plugged the Petbots in to charge, ready for the excitement of the next day.

## Chapter 10

# A Star is Born

It was Saturday . . . competition time!

'Time to get Charlie ready, so Mum and Dad don't get suspicious,' said Sophie. 'Anya and I will get him brushed and into the pet carrier.'

'We'll prepare up here,' said Archie. 'Let us know when you're ready for the switch.'

Sophie and Anya headed downstairs and

Archie, Flo and Sparky discussed the plan.

'Flo, you can watch the competition from where you were before, up above the stage, and warn us if you see anything suspicious.'

'Yes, boss,' said Flo.

'Sparky, you stick with Jack and keep an eye on the signal from my transmitter. I'll use the intercom to give you instructions.'

'Yes, boss.'

'I'll activate the transmitter as soon as we arrive so you can use it to track me. Okay, any questions?'

'I don't think so. We'll be playing it by ear really, won't we?' said Flo.

'Absolutely,' agreed Archie. 'We just need to stay focused and see what happens.'

Anya dashed in.

'Sophie's mum is outside loading the car – it's time to go.'

Flo flew out of the window, ready to follow the car to the theatre, and Anya, Archie and Sparky went downstairs to find Sophie.

She was standing in the hall with Charlie in his pet carrier on the floor. 'Ready?' she asked. Sophie tipped the big black-and-white cat out of

the carrier, Archie nipped inside, stuck his paws through the holes in the bottom and they wheeled the carrier into the front garden, leaving a surprised-looking Charlie sitting in the middle of the floor.

'Do you want me to take that?' Sophie's mum asked as they came out of the front door. 'Charlie's quite a lump.'

'No, it's fine, Mum,' Sophie said quickly. 'I've got him.'

They waited for Sophie's mum to get in and shut the door, then Sophie wheeled the carrier down the path and Archie extended his legs to get into the car.

'Off we go then,' said Mrs Stuart. 'Isn't this exciting!' She drove off down the road, Flo following up above.

When they got to the theatre Jack was waiting outside. Curiously, he had Buster in tow.

'Morning!' he said, glancing at the pet carrier in the back of the car. 'How's Charlie doing?' Jack bent down for a proper look and instantly had to clamp a hand over his mouth to stifle a laugh. It wasn't that the costume looked bad, it was more the expression on Archie's face. He really didn't seem to be enjoying the dressing-up part of the plan. Buster instantly recognised Archie's smell and got very excited, but when he looked in the carrier he was rather confused.

'Mum's just going to sign us in,' said Sophie, giving him a nudge.

'Er, okay,' he said, pulling himself together.

When Sophie's mum had left, they put the cat carrier onto the ground and Anya took the opportunity to transfer Sparky into Jack's pocket.

'Why on earth have you brought Buster?' she asked.

'Believe it or not, there are so many contestants missing that the show rang me last night to say he's on standby. Mind you, they said we would only have to perform as a last resort.'

Sophie was beginning to get nervous. 'I hope the plan goes well. I never actually practised the act yesterday with Archie, there wasn't time.'

'Don't you think your mum's going to notice that Charlie looks a bit, er, different?' said Jack.

'She'll be sitting in the audience because she wants to watch the performance,' Sophie said. 'I'm just hoping that the costume will be convincing enough to fool her. Anya's coming backstage with me.'

'Good idea,' said Jack.

Once they'd been signed in, Mrs Stuart went to find herself a seat near the front of the theatre. Sophie, pulling 'Charlie' in the cat carrier, Anya, Jack and Buster were led through to the dressing rooms backstage and found a quiet corner together away from the other contestants.

Meanwhile, Flo had taken her place up on the lighting rig, and was scanning the audience below.

'Archie,' she said over their intercom, 'do you read me?'

'Loud and clear!' replied Archie. 'I'm switching the transmitter on now, are you getting the signal?'

Flo could hear a quiet *beep, beep*. An image, like an aircraft control display, appeared in her visual sensor. A blinking dot corresponded with the beeps.

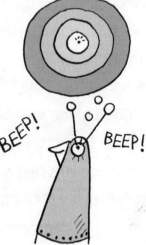

'Yep!'

'How about you, Sparky?'

'Loud and clear, boss,' he replied.

'Excellent!' said Archie. 'Flo, can you see anything unusual?'

'I'm scanning the crowd now,' Flo answered. She zoomed in on the faces below and almost instantly spotted the little old lady who owned the pet shop. 'Peggy's here,' she reported.

'What's she doing?' asked Sparky.

'Not much, just sitting in the audience, reading a magazine called *Pets Monthly*. Hey! Wait a minute,' she said, zooming in to maximum magnification, 'one of the pages has bits cut out of it, as if . . .'

'As if someone has cut letters out for a petnapper's note?' suggested Archie.

'Exactly!' said Flo.

'Keep watching, Flo,' said Archie. 'I'll tell the others.'

It wasn't long before the *Pet Factor* judges and presenters were ready, and the live semi-final was about to start. Fortunately enough contestants had turned up, so Jack and Buster were off the hook. Sophie and Anya had decided to keep Archie in the carrier until the very last minute, in case anybody looked at him too closely. When he stuck a paw out they huddled around the carrier and he told them about Peggy and what Flo had seen.

'So it was Peggy after all!' cried Jack.

'It certainly looks that way,' said Archie. 'Jack, I think you should take Buster and Sparky and sit in the audience – keep watch from there.'

Jack took Buster and set off right away.

'Good luck,' he called back. 'Break a leg!'

'Why would I want to do that?' asked Archie.

'It's just an expression,' said Sophie. She was beginning to get really nervous now. 'You do know what to do when we get on the stage, don't you, Archie?'

'Yes, don't worry,' he told her. 'I've been studying.'

Suddenly there was a burst of music from the auditorium: the show had begun.

As the contestants performed one by one Archie and the girls could hear cheers and applause from the auditorium, Sophie knew she and Archie weren't due to go on until the end of the first half, and the longer Sophie waited, the more nervous she became. By the time an organiser

came to find them, she was trembling like a leaf.

'Ready for you in five minutes,' said the stage manager.

'Okay,' said Sophie in a shaky voice.

'You'll be fine,' Anya told her and gave her a hug.

They lifted the lid of the carrier up and Archie got out for the first time. Sophie and Anya looked at him.

In Sophie's room, the homemade cat costume had looked quite convincing, but here, in the harsh light of the dressing room, it didn't look quite so good.

'This is never going to work!' panicked Sophie.

'It's okay,' said Anya with conviction, 'he just needs a bit of a brush.' She picked up Charlie's brush and fluffed up the fur fabric a bit.

'Careful of my whiskers,' Archie whispered.

'They're highly sensitive precision equipment!'

'Sorry, Archie.' She stood back to take a look. 'There, that's better.'

Archie looked in the dressing-room mirror.

'How did I ever get myself into this?' he wondered.

'Come on then,' said Sophie, 'it's now or never.'

They all stood in the wings, and Archie practised his cat moves as they waited. He was getting very good.

The footballing pig scored his final goal and received polite applause, then Sophie and Archie were ushered onto the stage and Phil the presenter introduced them. Sophie walked over to the piano and Archie sat beside her. Out in the audience, Mrs Stuart peered up at her daughter and the family cat who had just taken the stage – Charlie looked different somehow.

'I must get my eyes checked,' she said to herself, giving them a rub.

Sophie began to play. They'd decided to perform something a little more ambitious than 'Three Blind Mice' and had chosen 'The Animals Went in Two by Two'.

Archie soon joined in, pressing a few random keys with one paw at first. The audience clapped and laughed but Archie knew that this performance had to be a really good one to catch the petnapper's attention. So he decided to use both paws, and also that he should play notes in the same key as Sophie.

The audience were amazed. The judges were smiling.

Sophie looked at him, alarmed.

'Don't make it too good,' she whispered.

Anya watched anxiously from the side of the stage.

But Archie was getting carried away with the moment. He'd discovered that playing piano was really quite good fun and soon he began to copy what Sophie was actually playing. It sounded fantastic!

The audience were in uproar now. Flo was alarmed, and tried to contact Archie on the petbot intercom.

'Archie, stop! You're supposed to be a cat, not a concert pianist! This is on live television, you'll give us away!'

Sophie, frozen with confusion about what to do, had stopped playing and Archie was now performing solo. Flo was watching Peggy – if her jaw dropped any further, it would be on her lap.

'Archie!' whispered Sophie, nudging him as hard as she could, but he didn't respond – it was as if he'd been hypnotised by the music. Then she remembered what he'd said about his whiskers and she gave them a flick.

'Ow!' said Archie, but it worked, suddenly he remembered where he was. 'Er . . . meow!' he added, and stopped playing.

'Quick!' said Flo over the intercom. 'Get off the

stage, before anyone comes for a closer look.'

Archie trotted off into the wings. Sophie took a quick embarrassed bow and followed. The audience and the judges were on their feet, clapping and cheering and shouting 'Encore!' The only person not standing up was Sophie's mum, who sat stunned in her seat, wondering what on earth was going on.

'Peggy's on the move, Archie,' said Flo. She watched the little pet shop owner hastily make her way to the backstage door. 'Action stations. And by the way,' she went on, 'what was that?'

'Sorry, Flo, I got caught up in the moment! Who knew playing piano was so much fun?'

Archie had just got back into the carrier when Peggy poked her head round the door. She was clutching her clipboard and trying to look official.

'Hello there, dear!' she said. 'What a wonderful performance! The producers are asking for you out front. Shall I look after little Charlie while you're gone?'

Sophie suspected what Peggy was up to, but she played along, knowing that it was part of their plan too.

'Oh, okay, thank you, you're very kind.'

She left the room and signalled to Anya who was waiting in the corridor outside. They hid round the corner to watch what Peggy would do next.

Inside the dressing room, Peggy was addressing 'Charlie'. 'You're coming with me,' she said. 'No one's going to beat my Chico!' Moments later she emerged from the dressing room pulling the pet carrier, impressed that it had wheels – she didn't stock any like that in her shop and she imagined they would sell like hot cakes if she did.

'There she goes,' said Sophie.

Peggy pulled the pet carrier back into the auditorium; Anya and Sophie followed at a safe distance. They waved at Jack, sitting in the audience with Buster and Sparky. Flo watched everything from above.

'She's heading for the door,' said Flo. 'Sparky, are you ready to follow them?'

Sparky was already on his way, but it was an advert break so the cameras were turned off and the audience were getting up to stretch their legs.

It was almost impossible for him to navigate a path through the tangle of feet.

Peggy had almost reached the door by fighting her way through the audience and pushing the carrier in front of her like a battering ram. From her perch, Flo could see that Sparky was being left behind.

The old woman burst through the theatre exit, hurried to her van, which was parked close by, then picked up the carrier so she could shove it into the back of the van. She was in such a rush she didn't notice Archie using his extendable legs to support his weight and lift himself inside. Peggy jumped into the front seat and slammed the door. The tyres screeched as she drove away from the theatre at top speed.

Sparky raced out of the theatre just in time to

see the van disappearing round the corner. 'Flo, the van's left with Archie in it, I'm following.'

Sparky zoomed after the van in hot pursuit, keeping to the side of the road to avoid being squashed by traffic. Jack and Buster had been following Sparky, so Jack jumped on his bike, Buster running along behind. The young puppy loved chasing Jack on his bike, so for him the day was getting better and better, but by now Jack had lost sight of Sparky and had no idea which way to head. Luckily Flo flew down and sat on the handlebars.

'You pedal, Jack,' she said. 'I'll tell you where to go.' She paused for a second to locate where the transmitter signal was heading, then pointed a metal wing. 'They went that way!' she said.

Meanwhile, up ahead, Sparky was desperately trying to catch up with the speedy van. Eventually it had to stop at a red traffic light.

'At last!' he said. 'I've found you, Archie.'

He zoomed up the wheel arch and underneath the van. The traffic lights were just changing as Sparky found himself a safe place to stow away in the engine compartment.

Flo, Jack and Buster were still following the signal from the transmitter. Flo had tried to contact both Sparky and Archie over the intercom but they were too far away. Jack was pedalling furiously and

Buster, ears flapping, was enjoying every moment of the chase, but there was no way they could catch up with the van. Suddenly Flo let out a shriek.

'The signal's gone!' she said in a panic. 'The transmitter must be out of range. I've lost them both!'

# Chapter 11

# Caged!

'What are we going to do?' asked Flo in a flap.

'Don't panic,' said Jack, continuing to pedal like a maniac in the direction they'd been heading.

'But I've lost the transmitter signal! What if something terrible has happened?'

'Fly up and see if you can spot the van from the air,' suggested Jack.

'Of course! Why didn't I think of that?' Flo said, relieved to be told what to do.

She took off, carefully scanning the horizon for the van. There was a lot of traffic in town on a busy Saturday afternoon and it seemed like nearly every other vehicle was a white van. Quickly, Flo accessed her memory banks for an image of Peggy's old van and input the image into her visual scanning system. Almost instantly, the system highlighted a van speeding along the back streets. 'Got you!' said Flo.

'I've found the van!' she said, swooping down to Jack. 'Follow me.'

Jack pedalled furiously to keep up as she soared

back into the sky. Now it was Buster's turn to hitch a ride – his little puppy legs were worn out! He hopped up into Jack's bike basket gratefully.

Back at the theatre, the advert break was over, the cameras were rolling again and the next act was about to go on. Sophie and Anya had joined Mrs Stuart in the audience.

'How's Charlie?' she asked.

'Exhausted. He's sleeping like a baby so we left him backstage,' Sophie answered, less than truthfully.

'I'm not surprised,' said her mum. 'That was incredible! However did you teach him to play like that?'

Sophie smiled a little awkwardly but didn't say anything.

'It's agony not knowing what's happening out there,' Anya whispered to her friend.

'I know,' she agreed. 'I hope we hear something soon.'

'Charlie's sure to get through to the final!' Mrs Stuart went on.

'Yes, I expect he will,' agreed Sophie. But inside she was worried 'Charlie' might not come back at all.

Peggy's van was parked outside a small row of houses on the far edge of town. Peggy had pulled the pet carrier out of the car in such a hurry that she hadn't noticed Archie's feet sticking out of the bottom. She bumped and bashed the carrier downstairs into the basement, giving Archie a rather uncomfortable ride as he tried to half wheel and half walk himself down the steps. Sparky followed them, zipping through the basement door just before it swung shut. It was dark, shadowy and rather smelly in the basement.

'Here you are, my little piano-playing friend: welcome to your new home.' Peggy turned on the lights and the two Petbots found themselves in a room filled with cages. Every cage contained one of the missing acts from the *Pet Factor* competition. The imprisoned pets all noticed

Archie immediately, and the room suddenly became rather noisy. Peggy opened an empty cage and shooed Archie out of his carrier. 'In you go!' she said. Archie obeyed quietly and before he knew it she'd slammed the cage door shut and fastened it with a large padlock. He watched as she placed the key, together with lots of others, on a large keyring and hung it up by the door. 'See you later, Charlie. Shut up you lot,' Peggy said and went back upstairs.

'Sparky! Good to see you,' said Archie as Sparky whizzed across the room towards him. He zipped through the bars and did a figure of eight around Archie's front paws. The journey had worn the little mouse's batteries out, though, and he could feel his charge beginning to drain. Down here in the dark he wasn't getting any power from his solar panels either. 'Where's Flo?' asked Archie.

'I don't know,' said Sparky. 'She's with Jack and Buster but we got separated.'

Archie looked around the room. It was filled with some very miserable pets, some of whom he recognised from the *Pet Factor* videos that Flo had been watching.

There was a pitiful-looking python in the cage next to Archie.

'What did the python do, Sparky, do you remember?'

'Its owner did a snake-charming thing, I think,' said Sparky, 'then it wrapped its owner up like a sausage and rolled around the stage to music.'

'I remember the acrobatic monkey over there,' said Archie.

'That's right, Marvin the monkey!' said Sparky. 'And look, the pigeon circus from Charlie's first audition.'

Also in the basement were Lucy the llama who could count, three parrots – one which kept singing the same song over and over – several dogs, a couple of cats, a goat, a pig and a wallaby. Quite a collection!

'First things first,' said Archie, 'let's get these cages open. We could do with Flo being here, her beak would cut through the padlocks like a knife through butter.'

'My laser eyes,' suggested Sparky, 'they'll do it.'

'Great!' said Archie.

Sparky set to work on the first cage in the row, which held the acrobatic monkey. He was still wearing his stage costume that said 'Marvin' across the chest.

'Stand back, Marvin,' Archie advised him. At first the monkey didn't move, but when he saw the lasers begin to work, he fled to the far corner

of the cage. Sparky's lasers cut off the padlock with ease, but as it fell to the ground the smallest Petbot realised that there was a big problem.

'Archie, I'm almost out of charge!'

'Unlock my cage next, before you run out,' said Archie as a very excited monkey burst from his cage and started performing cartwheels around the room.

'Free at last!' thought Marvin. 'Free at last!'

Sparky tried to use his lasers but it was no good – he didn't have enough power. It wasn't working.

'Oh no! Sorry, Archie, why didn't I do your cage first?' moaned Sparky.

'It's not your fault,' said Archie. 'See if you can push that bunch of keys off the hook and bring it over to me.'

'Okay, I'll try.' Sparky did his best but he used almost all his remaining energy climbing up the wall and was too weak to push the heavy bunch of keys off the hook. 'Oh no!' he wailed again. 'What are we going to do?'

Archie was trying to think of a new plan but it was hard to concentrate with a monkey bouncing around the room. Then he had an idea.

'Hey, what about Marvin? Show him what to do.'

Sparky had just enough power to whizz around the monkey's feet and attract his attention. Intrigued by the little metal mouse, the monkey watched him run over to the keys and try to push them off the hook. As he watched, Archie realised why people used the saying 'Monkey see, monkey do'. Marvin pushed at the keys. He liked the sound

they made when they
jingled. Then he took
them off the hook.

'Hooray!' cheered
Archie and Sparky.
The monkey liked
them cheering and
jumped up and down
enthusiastically.

'Come here, Marvin, bring them to me,' Archie
said. To his delight, Marvin walked over to
Archie's cage, dragging the keys behind him.

Marvin had never seen a talking cat before.
The monkey looked at Archie, and tilted his head
to one side. Archie pointed at the keys, then at
the lock, hoping Marvin would understand what
to do. Sparky watched helplessly from the side

of the room, trying to conserve what little energy he had left so he wouldn't power down completely.

'I can't show you,' Archie said, frustrated, 'my paws won't fit through the bars.' Marvin looked at the keys, the padlock and then Archie – and finally the penny dropped. Archie pointed to the last key on the ring, the one that Peggy had just added, and shook the padlock.

Marvin was excited now – he had seen the old lady locking and unlocking the cages and he knew exactly what to do. He placed the key in the padlock and turned it. Immediately the padlock opened and fell to the ground.

'Marvin, you're a genius!' said Archie.

Marvin wasn't behaving much like a genius, though, he was doing more cartwheels and somersaults in celebration of his newfound talent.

Now that Archie was free he went to each cage in turn, unlocking padlocks until every animal had been freed.

'What now?' asked Sparky.

'Good question,' Archie replied. He was slightly worried that this particular mixture of livestock might not be a good one but at the moment the pets were all so happy to be out of their cages that it was all they cared about. 'If we can get the animals back in the van, we could take them back to the theatre.'

However it was at this point that the relative calm in the basement came to an abrupt end. One of the dogs decided it was time to chase one of

SQUAWK!

SPI

WOOF!

MEEOOW!

the cats. The parrots flapped out of the way and began to squawk loudly. The goat – spooked by the squawking – head-butted the door, and Marvin the monkey screeched at the top of his voice, jumping all over the empty cages and chucking around anything he could find. The sound was deafening, but even so,

ISSS!

OINK!

SQUAWK

Archie, with his radar ears, could hear footsteps coming downstairs.

'Peggy's coming!' he said, darting next to the door, ready to pounce. Sparky wheeled himself slowly over to the corner, safely out of the way.

The door flew open.

'What on earth is going on down here?' shouted Peggy above the din. The sound of loud cha-cha music was drifting down from upstairs.

Quick as a flash Archie darted forward, meaning to shove Peggy into the largest of the cages (which until recently had been occupied by a large hairy llama). Unfortunately he skidded on a pool of llama spit, slid across the floor and went crashing into the wall.

The Petbot struggled to his feet, tangled up in his soggy cat costume, and turned to see Peggy looming over him with a large net.

'You're no cat!' she said. 'I knew there was something fishy about you! So what exactly are you?'

# Chapter 12

# Breakout!

For a moment Archie thought that he was going to be caught, and his real identity revealed. Peggy could see his metal body shining through the holes in his costume and was beginning to realise that Archie was some sort of bionic pet. Then he noticed what was happening behind her, raised a metal eyebrow and pointed a paw. She turned round.

'Aarrgghh!!' screamed Peggy. The very large, angry python had crept up behind her. She panicked, dropping the net and backing away terrified. 'Help!' she shouted.

Marvin, now on a roll, picked up the enormous net and with a big swish, ensnared Peggy from head to toe.

'Marvin, you're a marvel,' shouted Archie. He spotted a coil of rope in the corner, grabbed the end and began to wind it round Peggy.

Chico the Chihuahua, who'd now followed his owner down to the basement, suddenly realised this might be his opportunity to escape the silly dog clothes and cha-cha practice. 'This is my chance for freedom!' he thought as he watched the other animals enjoying theirs. 'No more embarrassing costumes and no more stupid dancing!' Seized with the spirit of rebellion, he grabbed the other end of the rope and joined Archie in wrapping Peggy up like a parcel.

'No, Chico, no!' wailed Peggy.

'Yap, yap yap!' he replied.

Just then the animals heard excited barking coming from upstairs. Buster had followed Archie's scent! The puppy appeared in the basement, bounded over to his new friend and covered him in licks. Chico ran straight over to investigate. Buster and Chico hit it off straight away.

'Archie! Archie! Are you here?' came a familiar voice. 'We lost your signal!'

'Flo! Nice of you to join us!' said Archie.

She and Jack were at the top of the stairs. Seeing Archie, Flo flew down and wrapped both wings round him. Jack followed.

'Is Sparky with you?' a worried Flo asked.

'He's over there,' Archie told her, 'but he's almost out of charge.'

Jack ran through the roomful of animals, picked up the robotic mouse and held him gently.

'Hi there, Sparky,' he said. 'I'm so glad you're okay!'

Back at the theatre, *Pet Factor* was nearly over, and Sophie and Anya were worried. They'd heard nothing from any of the Petbots since Peggy had taken Archie.

'I'm going to show someone the letter,' Sophie said. 'I think it's time to call the police.'

'Maybe we should tell your mum first,' said Anya.

Sophie thought for a moment. 'I don't think she'd be too chuffed that I'd kept it quiet all this time.'

'Hmmm,' agreed Anya, 'I think you might be right.'

The girls found one of the backstage organisers and showed them Peggy's letter. They explained about Charlie being petnapped too – but left out the part about Charlie being impersonated by a robot cat.

'And you say Charlie was taken in a van?' said the man seriously.

'Yes, we think so. He disappeared over an hour ago,' said Sophie.

'And you're just telling us this now!' he exclaimed.

'Well, if you look at the note you can see why,' she explained.

The man pressed a button on his walkie-talkie. 'Get security down here right now,' he said. 'We have a situation.'

## Chapter 13

# Archie at the Wheel

Over at Peggy's house, Archie and Jack were herding the animals into the back of the van.

Peggy, tied up in the net with her feet sticking out from the bottom, was still protesting. Archie and Jack had helped her up the stairs and into the van with all of the animals.

'Get this net off me and untie me at once!'

'No can do, I'm afraid,' said Jack. 'Your number's up.'

It was a tight squeeze and the smell was far from pleasant. Archie's costume was gradually disintegrating, he'd lost one ear and part of his tail and there were a few tears here and there. Jack loaded Charlie's pet carrier on the floor by the front seat in case they needed it back at the theatre, put Sparky safely into his pocket and got on his bike.

'Er, who's driving?' asked Jack.

'Archie, of course,' said Flo, perching on top of the carrier. 'The Professor taught him, he's an excellent driver.'

Jack looked unconvinced.

'Just trust me, Jack, have I ever let you down before?' said Archie.

Jack relaxed – of course Archie had never let them down.

Marvin the monkey decided to climb in next to Archie and Flo, Buster and Chico joined them.

So it was that a very noisy van – with someone who looked a bit like a cat as its driver, a monkey and two dogs as the passengers and a metal bird acting as the satnav – made its way back to the theatre in the centre of town. Several drivers going in the opposite direction rubbed their eyes in disbelief as the Peggy's Pet Emporium van sped past.

The van drew up outside the theatre just as what seemed like half the local police force arrived. Sophie and Anya, watching from the foyer, ran outside.

'That's the van!' shouted one of the policemen, and instantly it was surrounded.

Archie ducked under the dashboard and Flo crept inside the pet carrier out of sight. Just then, Jack arrived on his bike and rode over to Anya and Sophie.

'The police!' he exclaimed.

'Yes,' said Sophie, 'we thought we'd better call them in case something had happened to you lot.'

'We have to get Archie and Flo out of there before the police search the van. Archie's costume is falling apart!' explained Jack.

'Was Archie *driving*?' asked Sophie.

'Yes,' said Jack. Sophie and Anya looked at each other in amazement, really impressed by Archie's skills.

Quite a crowd had now gathered outside the theatre, wondering what all the excitement was about. Most of them were pointing at Peggy's van – there was a tremendous banging coming from it. One of the policemen nodded to another and together they opened the back door. Out poured all of the animals, leaving Peggy inside, still wrapped in the net. There was a huge gasp from the crowd.

'That's her!' shouted Sophie. 'She's the petnapper!'

One of the policemen stepped forward.

'Madam,' he said, 'you're under arrest!'

'Under a net, more like,' laughed Jack.

Sophie saw her chance and ran towards the van.

'Keep back, Miss,' said a policeman, 'this is a crime scene.'

'But I can see my cat Charlie!' she wailed

dramatically. 'He's on the front seat, he'll be so frightened!'

'All right, Miss,' he said quietly, 'but be quick or I'll be in trouble.'

Sophie removed the carrier from the van and placed it on the ground, and opened it up. She saw that Flo was already hiding in the corner of it, and beckoned to Archie.

'Quick, Archie – get in,' she said, as soon as the policeman's back was turned. As quickly and carefully as she could, she wheeled the carrier over to the others. The van was empty now, except for

Marvin the monkey who was playing with the steering wheel.

'You don't think the monkey drove the van do you, Sarge?' one of the policemen said.

'Beats me,' the sergeant replied. 'Someone just told me that there's a cat that can play piano. I s'pose anything's possible!'

Back at Sophie's house later that evening, the Petbots, Sophie, Jack and Anya were watching a news report on the laptop. Charlie was curled up asleep on Sophie's bed. Sparky was next to him, plugged in and recharging. Buster was curled up next to Sophie having a well-earned rest. Chico was with them too – he seemed to have adopted them as his new owners.

'Look at Chico!' Sophie laughed.

He was happily chewing his Mexican coat and sombrero to shreds 'Ha ha! At last, no more stupid costume,' he growled to himself triumphantly.

'Police are still baffled as to how a van containing missing *Pet Factor* contestants reached the town's theatre this evening. The pets, who were stolen following their appearances on the  popular television show, have been reunited with their owners and the programme's producers are delighted that there has been a happy conclusion to the drama. The grand final will go ahead next

Saturday as planned, with most of the acts confirmed to appear again. Unfortunately, we are told that Charlie the piano-playing cat, who's already an Internet sensation after his appearance this evening, will not be appearing in the grand final after his petnapping ordeal. Local pet shop owner Peggy Scrimshaw, who performed under the stage name "Carmelita" with her dancing Chihuahua Chico, has been arrested and is likely to be charged in connection with the crime.

'In other local news, a man was taken to hospital and is being kept in for observation after crashing his bicycle into a pond. The man claims he lost control of the bicycle after he saw a cat driving a vehicle containing a monkey and a bird through the town centre earlier this afternoon.'

'Oops!' cried Archie.

'So the competition is back on track!' said Flo.

'Yes,' said Sophie, 'but Charlie and I have had enough of the limelight.' She stroked Charlie's ears gently and he started to purr. 'Anyway, I really don't think he could live up to Archie's performance so I had to pull out.'

'It certainly was a showstopper,' said Anya.

Archie grinned.

The following week was the *Pet Factor* live grand final. The Petbots gathered around their laptop in the school attic to watch the show. All of the kidnapped pets had been reunited with their owners and they all performed in the final. There was only one winner for the Petbots, though, and they all voted for him. It was of course Marvin the monkey!

**Don't miss these other Petbots adventures!**

# The Great Escape

ISBN: 978 1 84812 348 5

Meet Archie the cat, Sparky the mouse and
Flo the bird – three pets built by a brainy
professor to be the perfect robo-friends!
But without him, their quiet life is turned upside
down. The mechanical marvels are forced to
leave their house and use all of
their special robot powers to
survive the dangers of the
outside world. . .

# School Shutdown

ISBN: 978 1 84812 411 0

The Petbots love their new home in the school attic, but when a nasty computer virus races through the systems, causing mayhem and madness in class, and Archie starts acting strangely, Flo and Sparky start to wonder if Archie's caught something too. Can their new human friends save Archie from shutting down for good?

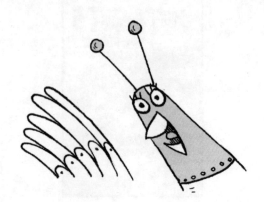

# piccadillypress.co.uk/children

Go online to discover:

☆ more authors you'll love

☆ competitions

☆ sneak peeks inside books

☆ fun activities and downloads